Just Like You

JAN FEARNLEY

To the memory of my father, Leslie Robertson. He was very, very special.
And for his grandchildren, David and Elizabeth.
Love and thanks to Genevieve and Ramona.

First published in Great Britain 2000

by Mammoth, an imprint of Egmont Children's Books Limited, a division of Egmont Holding Limited

239 Kensington High Street, London W8 6SA

Text and illustrations copyright © Jan Fearnley 2000

Jan Fearnley has asserted her moral rights

Hardback 0 7497 4577 0

Paperback 0 7497 4231 3

A CIP catalogue record for this title is available from the British Library

Printed in the UAE

10 9 8 7 6 5 4 3 2

It was dusk.

The red evening sun snuggled down to the hillside,
resting on purple pillows of clouds.

Mama Mouse and Little Mouse were making
their way home to bed.

As they walked along, they could hear the other animals talking quietly to their babies as they settled them down for the night.

Mama Bird was tucking her chicks into the nest. Carefully, tenderly, she smoothed their downy feathers.

"I will fly for you," she sang softly as they closed their little eyes. "I will fly as high as the clouds, across the skies, to find the finest food for you. That's what I will do."

"Isn't that lovely," said Little Mouse.

"Her babies must be very special."

"Yes, they are," said Mama Mouse.

"Just like you."

They came upon Daddy Frog.

He was tucking his froglets under a lily leaf.

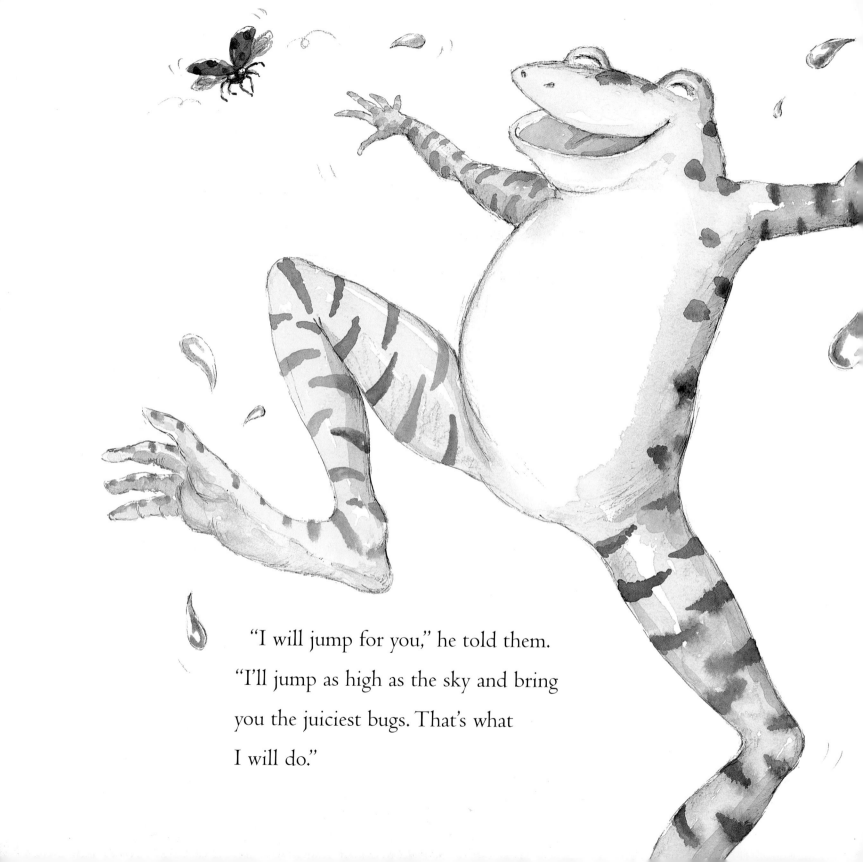

"I will jump for you," he told them. "I'll jump as high as the sky and bring you the juiciest bugs. That's what I will do."

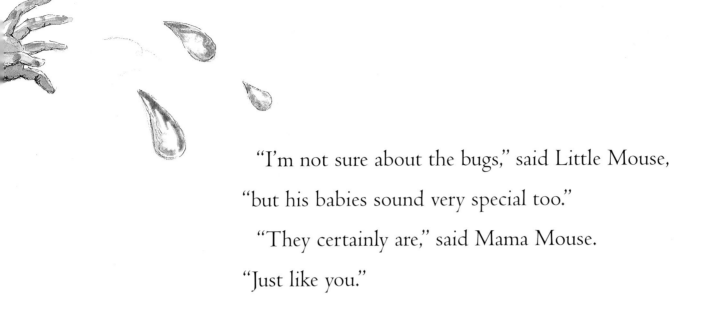

"I'm not sure about the bugs," said Little Mouse,
"but his babies sound very special too."

"They certainly are," said Mama Mouse.

"Just like you."

As they tiptoed through the grasses, they came upon
Mama Rabbit with her kittens, catching the last of the
sunshine.

"I will dig for you," she told them. "I will dig the deepest,
most secret burrow to keep you safe as treasure and warm forever.
That's what I will do."

"That's a lot of hard work," sighed Little Mouse.

"What special, special babies."

"Just like you," said Mama, squeezing his little paw.

As they walked along the seashore, they could
make out the sound of Mama Seal crooning to her pup.
They were settled on a bed of weeds as the waves lapped
a lazy lullaby against the shore.

"I will swim for you, my darling," she said. "I will dive as deep as the deepest ocean, and find you the sweetest of treasures: shells, corals and fish, whatever you wish. That's what I will do."

"Verrrry special," sighed Little Mouse.

"Just like you," reminded Mama.

But Little Mouse had a faraway look about him.

Wandering up the hillside, they saw Fox playing with his cubs.

"I will run for you," he said. "I will run as far and as fast as
ever I can and be clever and quick and cunning to keep you safe
from harm. That's what I will do."

Little Mouse looked very thoughtful.

Now they were home.
Mama Mouse gave her baby,
Little Mouse, a cuddle.

"It's time for bed," she said.

As he got ready, Little Mouse looked at his Mama
and said, "Mama, what will *you* do for *me*? You can't
fly, or jump high, you don't dig or dive and you can't
run as fast as a fox. You're only a little mouse. Am I
not as special, then?"

Mama Mouse smiled and
tucked her baby under the covers.
"Well, all that may be true," she said,
"but even a little mouse can do quite
a few things. Let me see . . .

I'll tell you stories to make you smile,

I'll find you nice things to nibble on,

I'll play with you and
make you laugh,

I'll hug you and keep you safe and . . .

. . . when you're naughty, I promise I'll be very, very
cross with you!

But most of all, I promise I will always love you and
care for you. And I'll do it with all of my heart."

Little Mouse smiled a sleepy smile.

"That's an awful lot. I must be very,
very special," he said.

"Yes, you are," whispered Mama,
dropping a kiss on his little furry head.

And as Mama Mouse tiptoed to the bedroom door,

Little Mouse whispered, "Just like you, Mama. Good night."